W9-BZB-250

THE ROCK

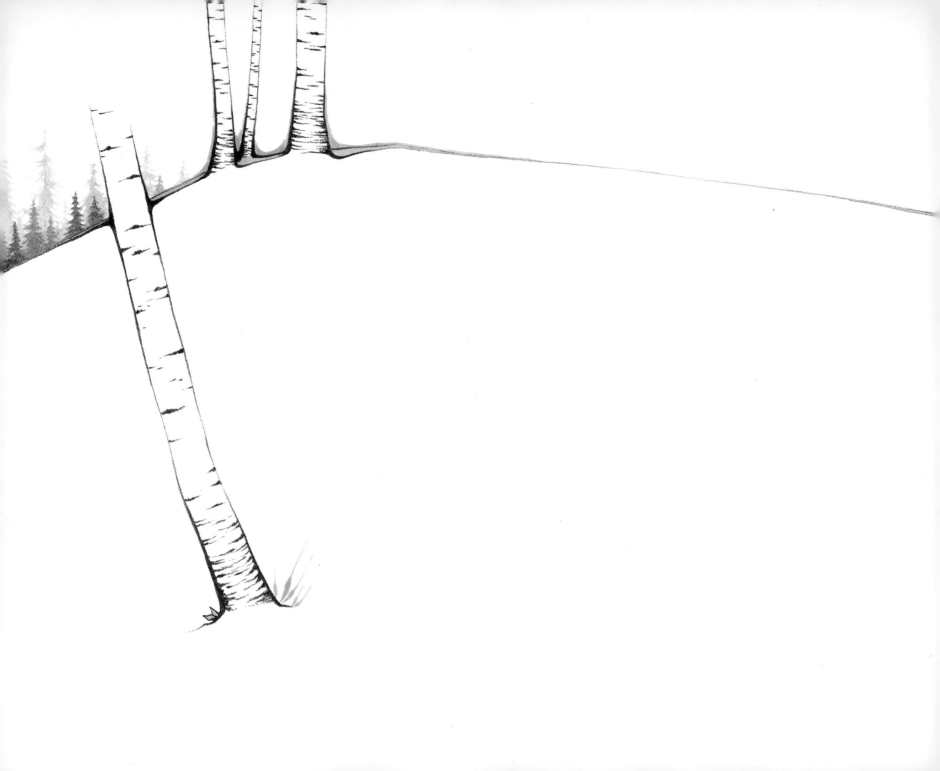

THE ROCK

WRITTEN AND ILLUSTRATED BY PETER PARNALL

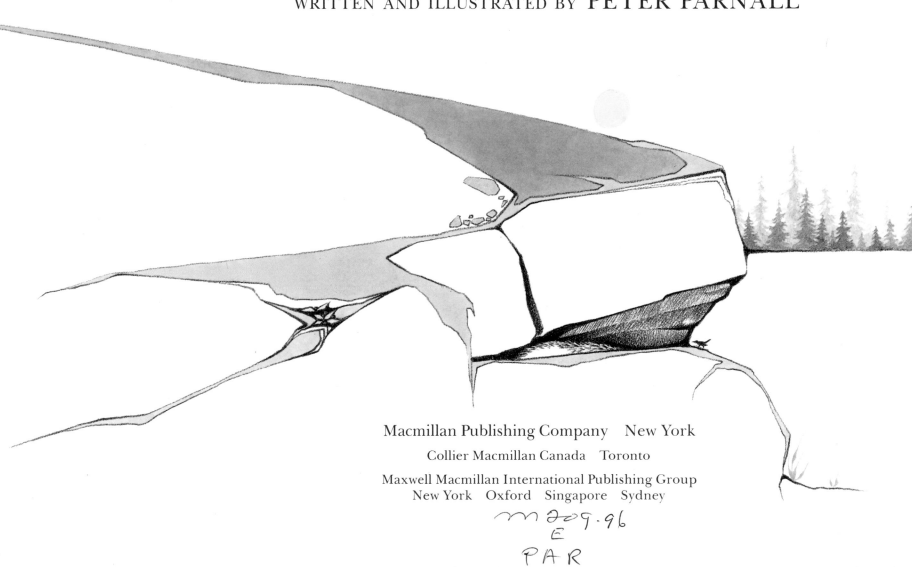

Macmillan Publishing Company   New York

Collier Macmillan Canada   Toronto

Maxwell Macmillan International Publishing Group
New York   Oxford   Singapore   Sydney

m 209.96
E
PAR

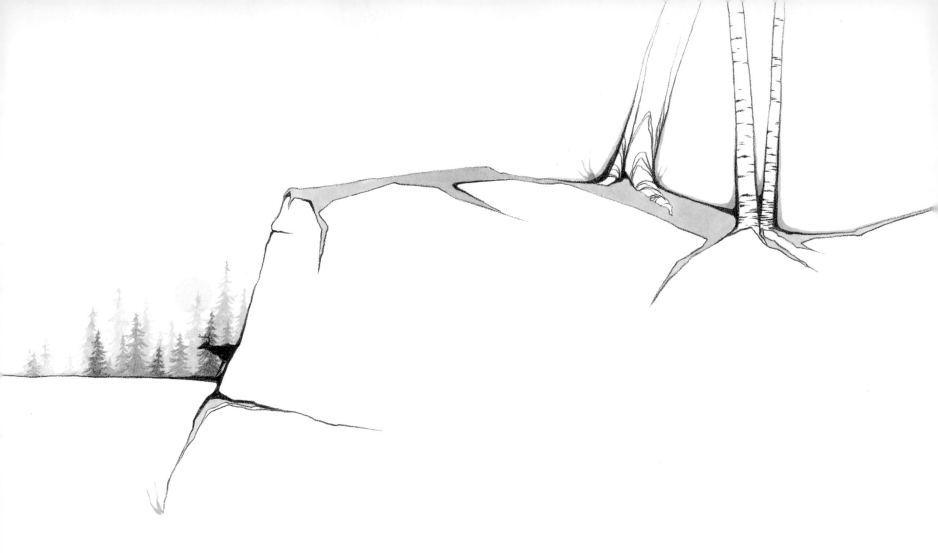

Copyright © 1991 by Peter Parnall · All rights reserved. No part of this book may be reproduced or transmitted
in any form or by any means, electronic or mechanical, including photocopying, recording, or by any information
storage and retrieval system, without permission in writing from the Publisher.
Macmillan Publishing Company,
866 Third Avenue, New York, NY 10022, Collier Macmillan Canada, Inc.
Printed and bound in Hong Kong   First Edition   10   9   8   7   6   5   4   3   2   1
The text of this book is set in 14 point Baskerville. The illustrations are rendered in pencil, watercolor, and ink.
Library of Congress Cataloging-in-Publication Data · Parnall, Peter. The rock/written and illustrated by Peter Parnall.
— 1st ed.   p.   cm. Summary: Over the years a rock provides homes, shelter, food, and a place to sit for visiting
animals and people.   ISBN-0-02-770181-6   [1. Rocks — Fiction. 2. Forest ecology — Fiction. 3. Ecology — Fiction.]
I. Title. PZ7.P243Ro   1991   [E] — dc20   90-6021   CIP   AC

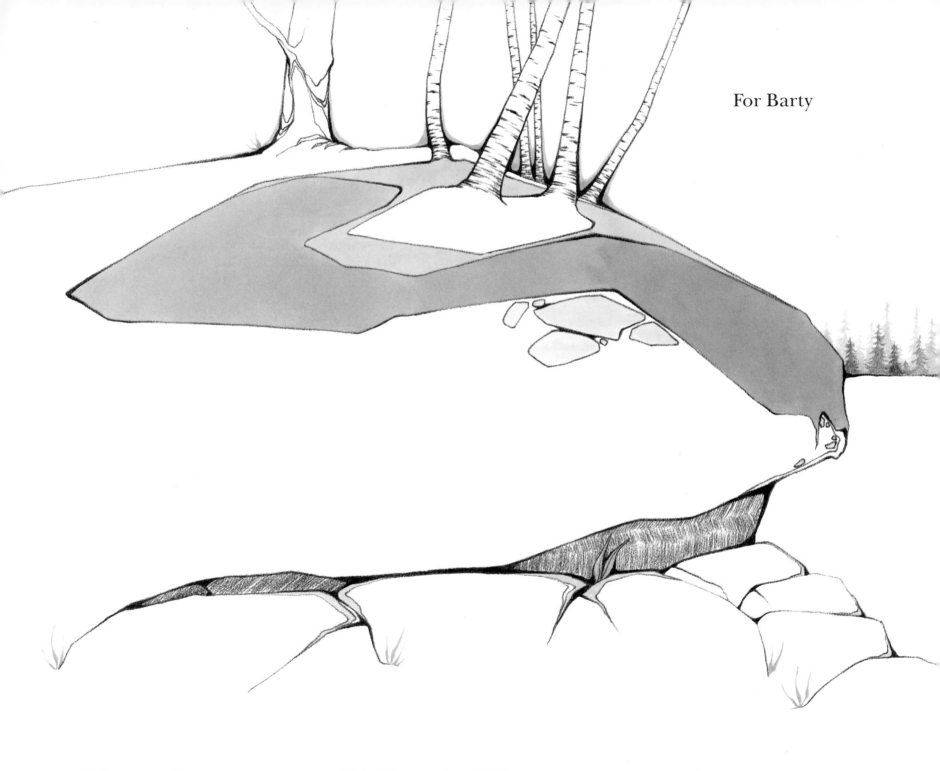

For Barty

To some, the Rock is just there; just a huge lump on the forest floor…in the way. It is furry with moss and lichens, and there are crevices along its gray, front face large enough to crawl into — away from the rain. I know, because I did it one day during a thunderstorm. In the front? To me it is the front. Where I sit is *always* the front. That's the side I sit by to watch Deer pick his way quietly through birches on his way to an evening's drink and a meal of tender buds. He spends his days in dark thickets of spruce, back beyond the pines. Thickets where Sun rarely reaches to the ground, and soft green plants never grow. Below the birches, in open sunny places, that's where buds and tender shoots wait for Deer.

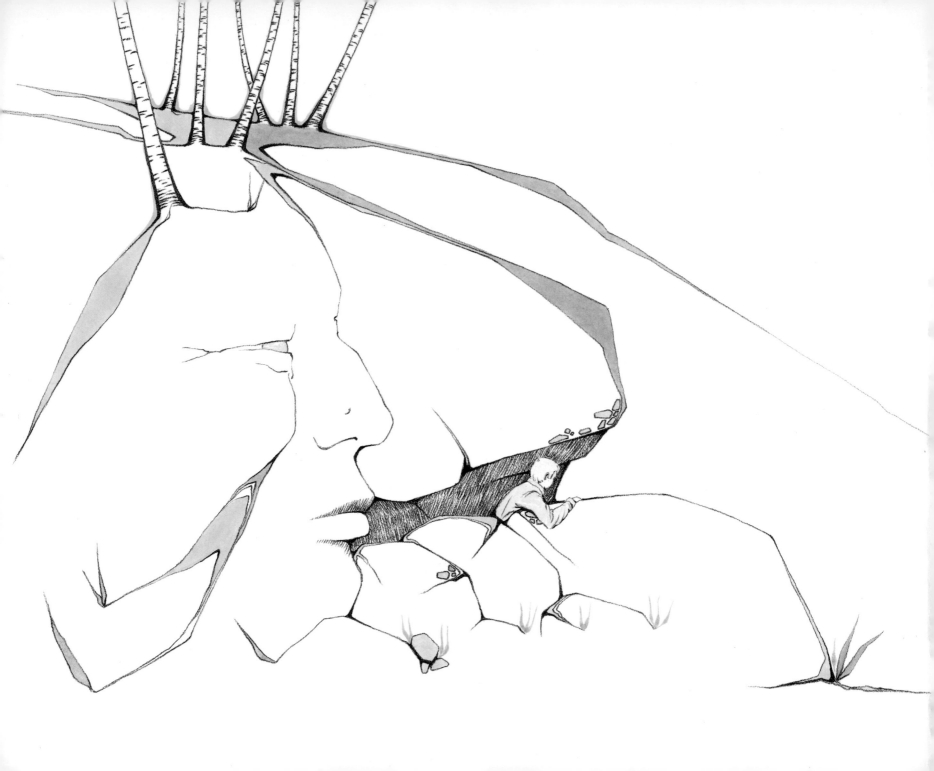

Fox discovered the Rock on a late afternoon hunt. In
September. Cricket month. This day, as she trotted
purposefully through the woods toward open fields
where crickets lived, she chose a new route, one through
thickets of tall, drying ferns. Thickets that in a wetter
season would have hidden Leopard Frog. But not now.
Fox's path took her alongside the part of the Rock where
I hide from the rain. The front. She sniffed the air, she
sniffed the ledge, she listened on tiptoe, then carefully
picked her way into the crevice—farther than I can go
—and discovered an old woodchuck den deep, beyond,
and out of sight of any prying eyes. She claimed it for
her own.

So did Indian. I can sense him here with me, here in the shadow of the Rock's west face, waiting for Deer as the sun goes down. When green pine boughs slowly turned to blue, Indian listened for the scrape of an antler against a twig, a hesitant step, a breath, as Deer stepped out from the safety of thick spruce into the open pine forest, testing the air with nose and ear. Testing for dangers hidden along his path to a fresh, sweet drink. For many centuries many Indians have waited for Deer to come to the tiny pond fed from a spring, here, beneath the Rock.

Then went to the cricket field.

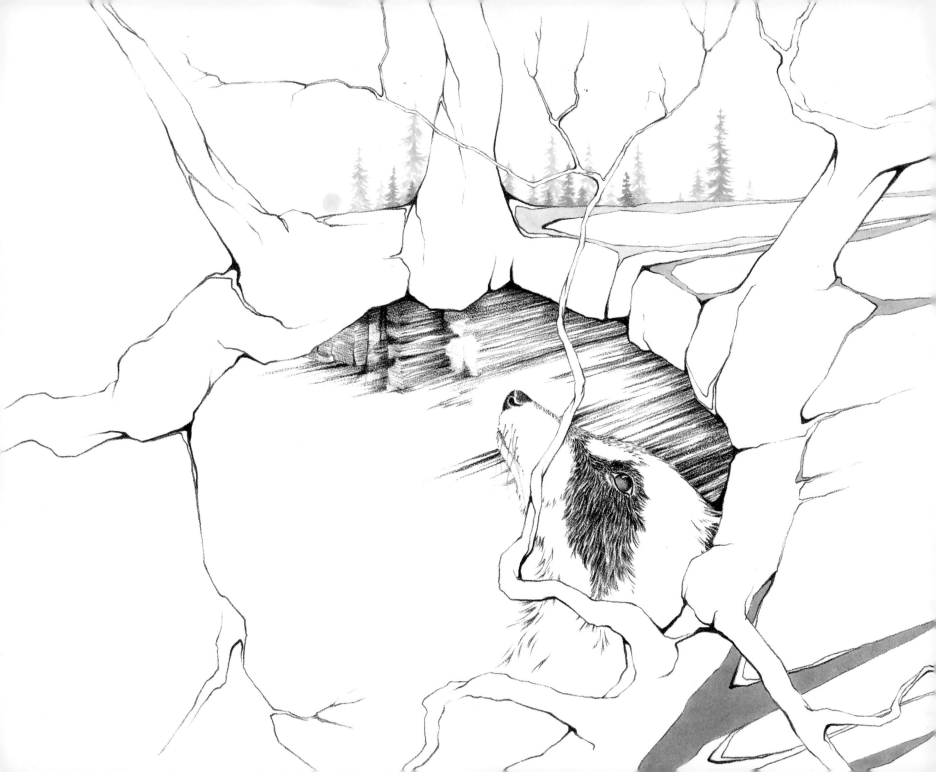

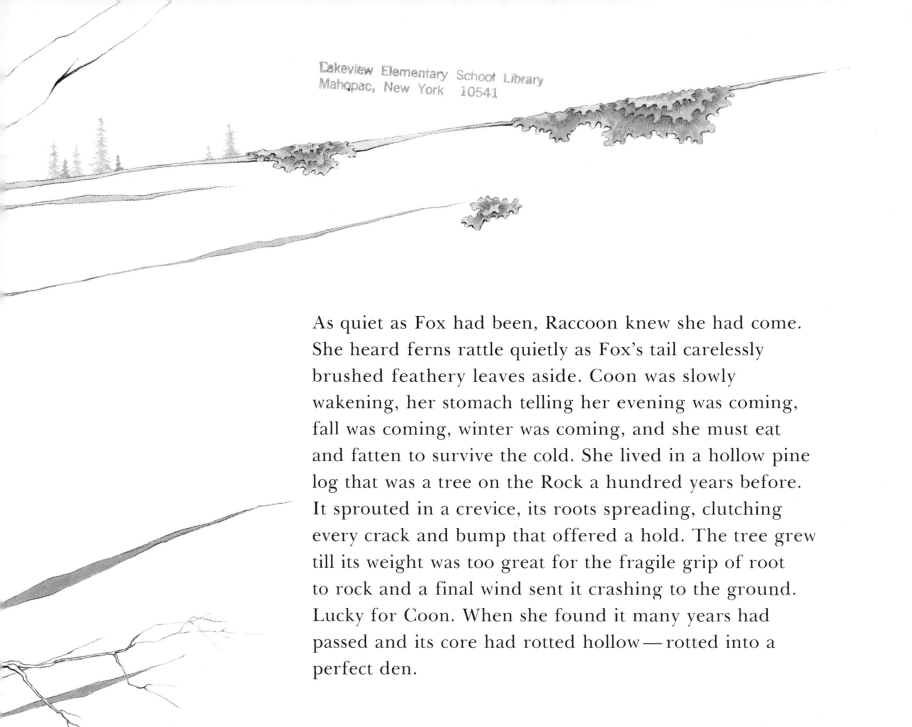

Lakeview Elementary School Library
Mahopac, New York   10541

As quiet as Fox had been, Raccoon knew she had come.
She heard ferns rattle quietly as Fox's tail carelessly
brushed feathery leaves aside. Coon was slowly
wakening, her stomach telling her evening was coming,
fall was coming, winter was coming, and she must eat
and fatten to survive the cold. She lived in a hollow pine
log that was a tree on the Rock a hundred years before.
It sprouted in a crevice, its roots spreading, clutching
every crack and bump that offered a hold. The tree grew
till its weight was too great for the fragile grip of root
to rock and a final wind sent it crashing to the ground.
Lucky for Coon. When she found it many years had
passed and its core had rotted hollow—rotted into a
perfect den.

Hawk found it, too. One large root reached for the sky,
and he perched there, watching for Squirrel or Mouse to
make a dash foolishly across the open, mossy carpet that
covers the Rock's upper parts. Usually they sense him
there, and worm their way through hidden paths in
crevices, niches, and cracks. The Rock is armor for some.

Some lucky ones.

Moose came to the Rock one fall, attracted by the smell of overripe apples scattered beneath a stunted tree: a tree struggling to grow on a granite bed. He ate them all, then ate the tree (well, the good parts), then discovered Hawk's rooty perch and rubbed his antlers till some velvet fell, exposing hard, new horn. He usually rubbed on small firs and pine, but returned to the Rock a number of times to joust with the root of Hawk until it finally fell with a splintery crash. Neither Hawk nor Moose returned. Mouse didn't mind.

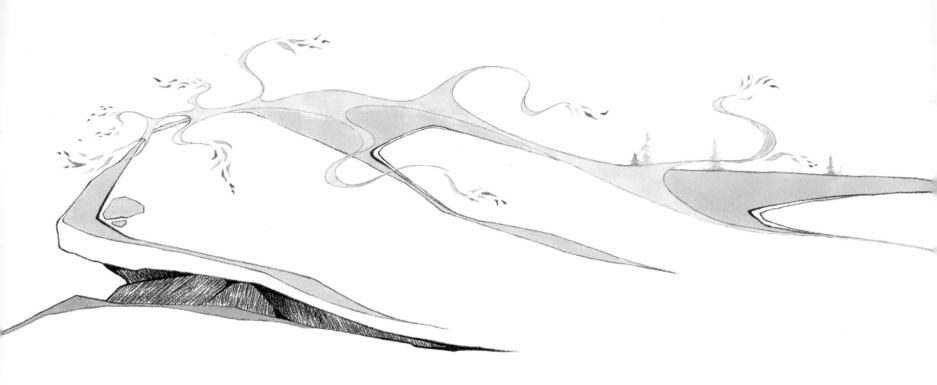

One very dry year lightning struck a tall black spruce
that grew straight upon the Rock's east side, setting fire
to the layer of moss and ferns that formed the Rock's
thick skin. Wind drove sparks in swirls of light till all that
grew on the great stone shape was flaming high. Fox fled
her heating den, and Mouse scurried for safety Beyond,
Away — to an unknown place. A place safer than fire.

The tiny pond was too small to protect Beaver. Beaver, whose family had been first to discover and use the trickling spring that rose from beneath the Rock's bones. The dam they made created this pond—a watery landmark for generations of creatures ruled by hunger and thirst. Beaver lumbered off to larger water, and a home safe from fire.

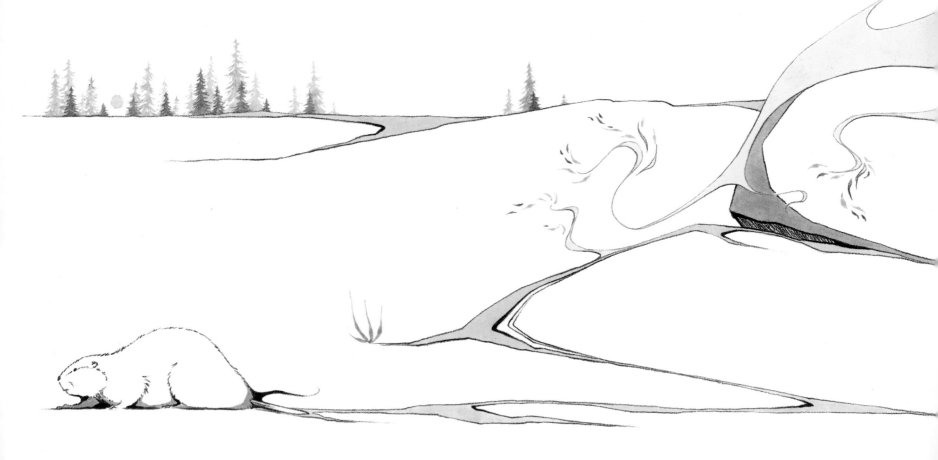

The Rock, blackened, stripped of its coat of spruce and
firs, lichens and ferns, no longer a home or shelter for
those who barked or squeeked, stood silent and dark
for years and years. Then, one day in June, a tiny shoot
struggled above the ashy soil. A shoot sprouted from a
wind-borne seed that lodged in a crack where Mouse
used to run.

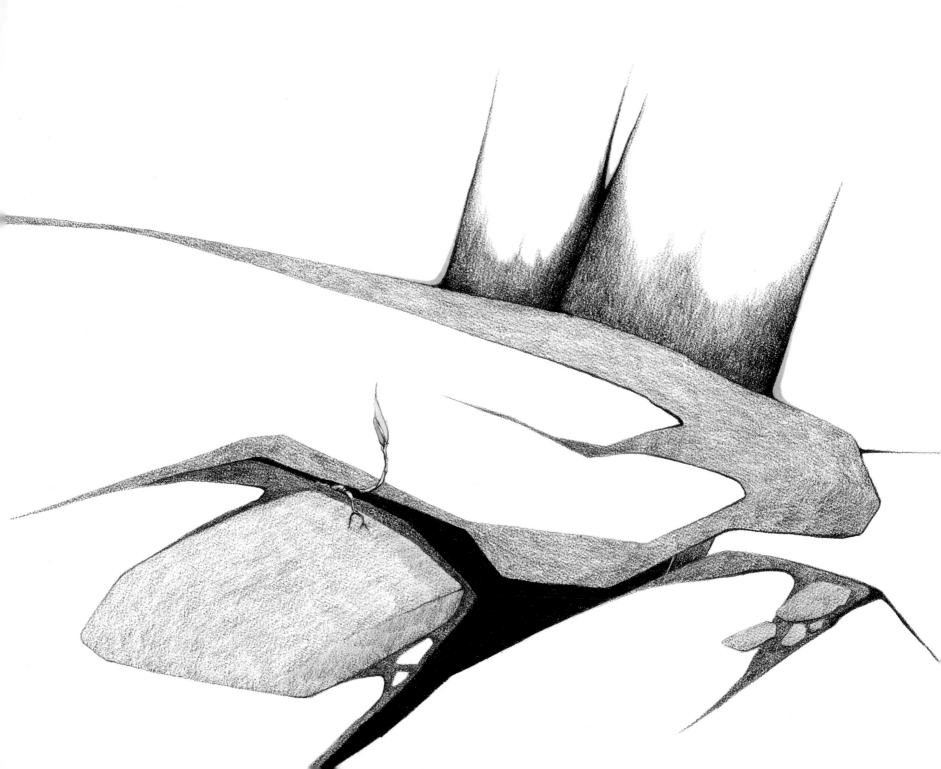

The top of the Rock, which before the fire had held only
shadows, moss, lichens, and ferns, now glowed in light.
And raspberries grew. Strawberries, too. And grass. And
Mouse. Deer came to feed on the Rock again. Hawk
came to watch... and listen.

A little boy came, too. He sat high, hidden in a clump
of birch, watching Beaver rebuild a long-dead dam. And
he saw Fox trotting through the ferns on her way to
Somewhere. Somewhere she knew fat crickets grew. The
boy imagined he was an ancient hunter, watching.

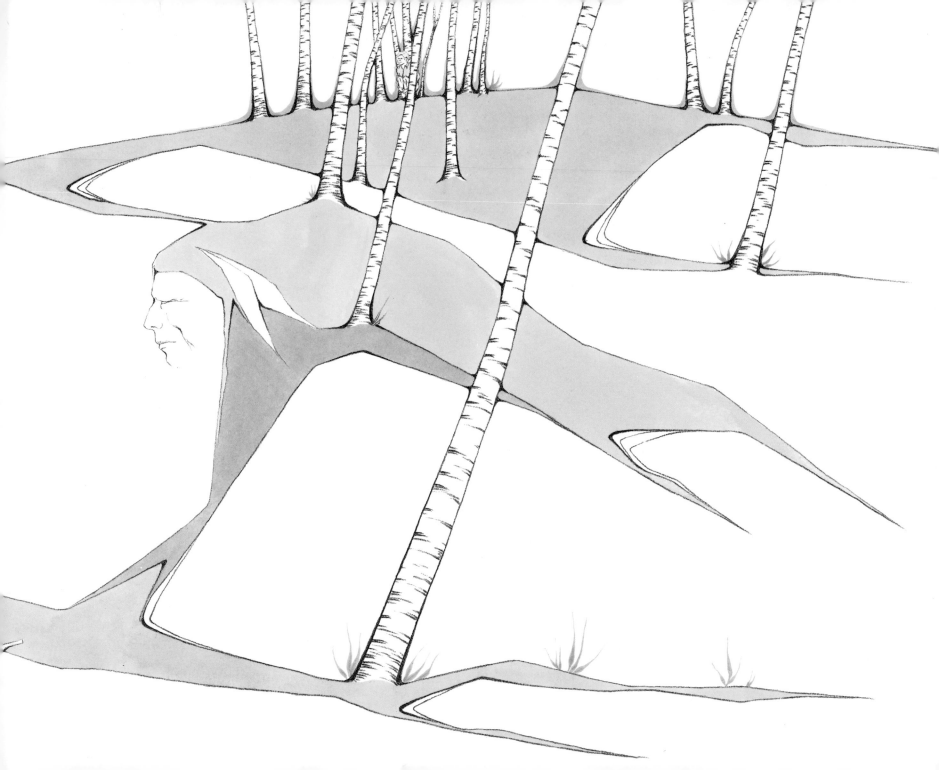

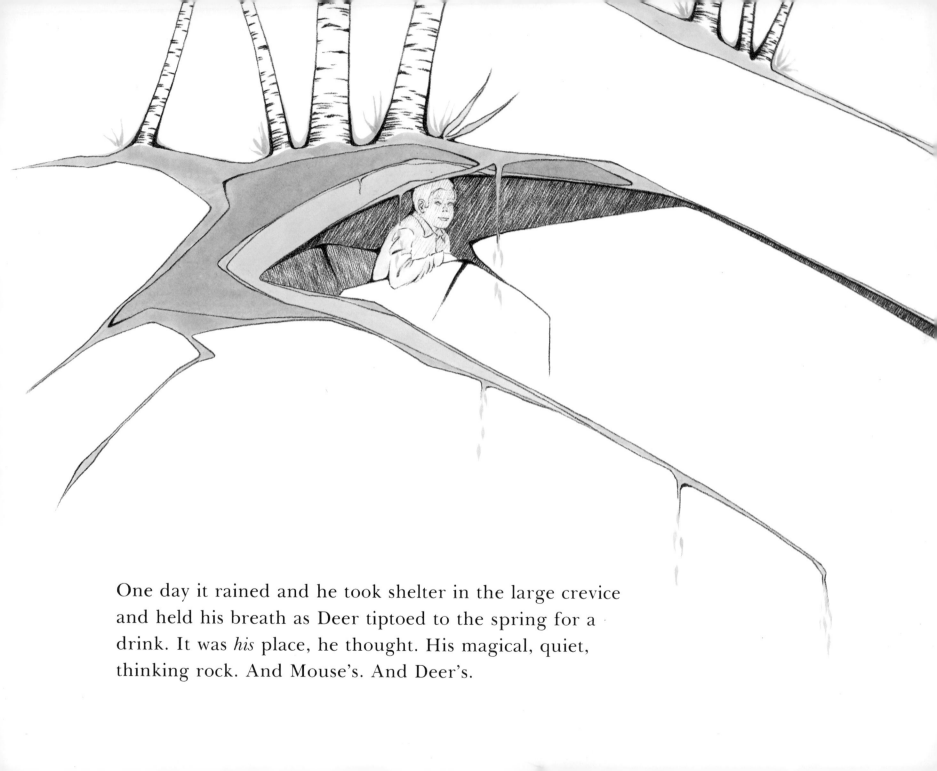

One day it rained and he took shelter in the large crevice and held his breath as Deer tiptoed to the spring for a drink. It was *his* place, he thought. His magical, quiet, thinking rock. And Mouse's. And Deer's.

Or maybe it belonged to anyone who would like to sit there...and watch.

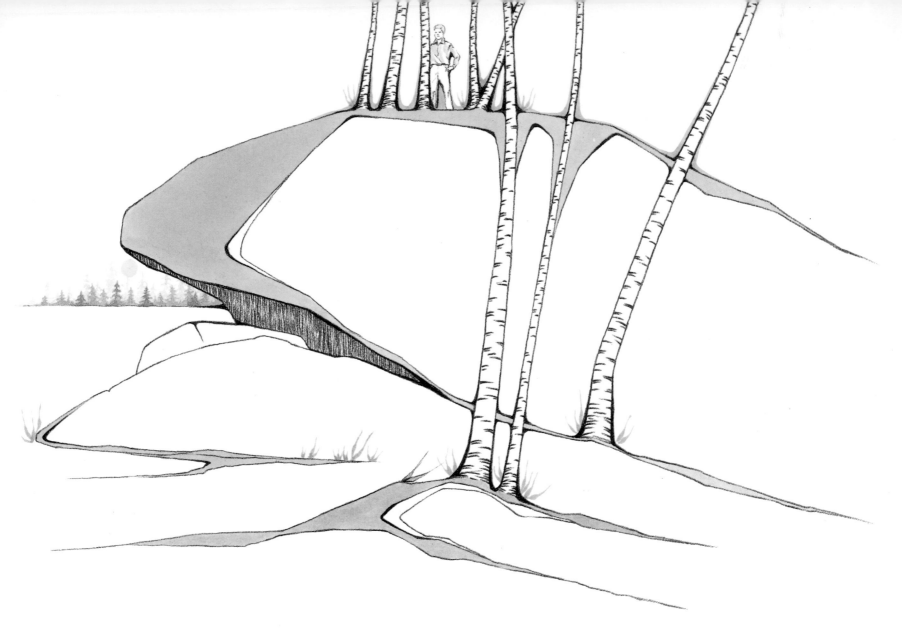

He thought it would be good to take care of it,

for the next guy.